The Mouse
— in the —
Hammock
a Valentine's Tale

by BETHANY BREVARD
art by MARCIN PIWOWARSKI

DREAM BIG PUBLISHING, LLC
AUSTIN, TEXAS

It happens this time every winter.

I slowly wake up in my cozy, warm hammock,

stretch my body and...**JUMP** out of bed!

I scurry to the window, and I look outside.

The sun is shining! The snow is melting!

Flowers are blooming! Everything looks lovely.

I see two doves hugging.

"AWWWWW!"

I see two squirrels dancing.

"AWWWWW!"

And I see two children holding hands.

"AWWWWW!"

I can feel it. Love is in the air.

And this can only mean one thing...

Valentine's Day is near!

That's a busy time for a **LITTLE** mouse like me. That's when
I get to show my friends just how much I love them.

On Valentine's Day, people give each
other presents, cards or chocolates
(or, all three, if they really, **REALLY** like you!).

But, I have none of these things.

How can someone **LITTLE** like me
show how **BIG** my heart is?

I'll have to get creative!

So I scurry around the house, looking for all of the **LITTLE** things that show I care!

The children's room is always a good place to start.

On the first day of February, I find a piece of scrap paper.

Hmm...what can I do with this?

I wonder.

I KNOW!

And I neatly fold it into an airplane.

Woosh!

You make my heart soar

On the second day of February,
I find a bear cookie.

Growl!

Hmm...what can I do with this?

I wonder.

You're the bear-y best!

I KNOW!

And I lay it on the table.

On the third day of February, I find a toy frog.

Hmm...what can I do with this?

I wonder.

Ribbit!

I KNOW!

And I tie my card to the frog.

On the fourth day of February,
I find a **LITTLE** toy car.

Zoom!

Hmm...what can I
do with this?

I wonder.

I KNOW!

And I skid it across
a piece of paper.

You're wheel-y cool!

On the fifth day of February,

I find an old stuffed monkey.

Hmm...what can I do with this?

I wonder.

I like hanging with you!

Ook, hoo, hoo, hoo!

I KNOW!

And I attach it to Monkey's toe.

With each passing day, I use all the **LITTLE** things I find to show my friends my love for them and I leave them around the house for them to discover.

From a rocket to a dinosaur.
From marbles to googly eyes.

Every morning I can hear them squealing
in delight as they find my **LITTLE** gifts.

And this makes me happy. Very happy.

For every smile, every laugh, every shriek of delight
makes my heart feel **BIGGER** and **BIGGER**.

Finally, Valentine's Day arrives.

I run around the house, looking for one last token to give
to my friends, but something else catches my eye.

The glow of a golden heart.

"This is for you," says the note.
"Thank you."

I hug the golden heart.

What a great gift!

How could I ever top it?

I KNOW!

No **LITTLE** gifts this
time. No notes,
no candies,
just me.

Because being there for my friends is the
greatest gift I could ever give them.

The best way to make friends is to simply be friendly.

LITTLE acts of friendship make a **BIG** difference!

'Tis the Night Before Valentine's Day

'Tis the night before Valentine's
And all through the house
Not a creature is stirring,
Except one little mouse...

Mouse has been waiting
All winter long,
Warm in his hammock,
Humming a song.

He's just so excited
For Valentine's Day,
The gifts people give,
The words people say!

But how can a mouse
Tell all his best friends
How much he loves them
Without treats to send?

Chocolates and roses
A mouse cannot buy.
"Oh, what should I do?"
The little mouse sighs.

But Mouse is creative.
An idea goes pop!
Through trinkets and trash,
For presents he'll shop!

The children's room
Is the messiest place,
So Mouse races over,
A grin on his face.

A scrap piece of paper
Lying on the floor?
Mouse folds an airplane:
You make my heart soar!

Look, here's a puzzle!
Mouse's luck increases!
It's the perfect message:
I love you to pieces!

A toy monkey, a tiny car,
And even a rusty key.
Marbles and noodles and googly eyes—
Mouse uses all of these!

In the morning, the children
Squeal with delight.
Mouse's love grows huge.
His heart takes flight!

But wait, what's this,
Glowing and gold?
It's a beautiful heart
That Mouse can hold!

This wonderful surprise
Is for Mouse, it's true!
It comes with a note
That says "Thank you."

Mouse is amazed.
What a special gift!
But how in the world
Could he EVER top this?

Suddenly he knows
Exactly what to do:
He climbs up on the table
And says, "I'm here for you!"

Our little mouse
Understands in the end
That the BEST gift is simple:
Just be a friend.

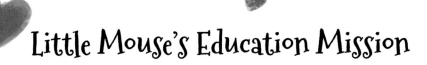

Little Mouse's Education Mission

Mouse is on a mission to teach you that, even though you are **LITTLE**, you can make a **BIG** impact in the lives of children all over the world.

By simply buying this book, you have given a donation to Lekol Lespwa, a school in Haiti that teaches over 40 children aged four to 18?

Thanks to your contribution, these children can study math, reading, science, as well as the Bible, in a safe learning environment.

We believe that education plays an important role in breaking the cycle of poverty, and for this reason, a portion of all the Mouse in the Hammock book sales goes to them. Just $1000 can fund this school for an entire month.

Thank you for being such a great friend to Mouse and the children of Haiti by buying this book and sharing it with your friends.

Lekol Lespwa (Hope School) is a partnership between TEEMHaiti, Maison des Enfant de Dieu and Alexis Foundation Haiti.

You can find out more at **www.teemhaiti.com**

A portion of the proceeds from all The Mouse in the Hammock books supports children in Haiti.

The Mouse
— in the —
Hammock
a Christmas Tale.

Can a little mouse with a **BIG** heart...make Christmas extra special? How will he get it all done?

The Christmas tree is decorated. Presents in bows and bright colors surround it. And stretched between two branches is a wool hammock. This is where our hero lives. He loves watching all the adults running around to make holiday preparations.

But there are some things getting missed.

Maybe he can help?

You and your children will love this adorable tale, because the Christian themes of Jesus and doing for others will teach them that every kindness matters.

Available at **www.TheMouseintheHammock.com**

Bethany Brevard is a wife, mom, entrepreneur and most recently, an award-winning children's book author. It is her goal to help any family experience the joy of making significant global impact through stories and hand-made plush ornaments.

1 John 4:11, NIV

"Dear friends, since God loved us that much, we also ought to love one another."

To J: Your unconditional love and friendship
is the greatest gift in my life. ♥B

Special thanks to Marcin: for understanding my crazy ideas
and transforming them into such beautiful loving images.

Thank you to my amazing team: Story Editor, Laura Caputo-Wickham,
Rhyming Editor, Michelle Turner, Layout Designer, Jodi Giddings,
and my mom, Marion Coleman. Thank you all for your
creativity, your rhyming expert skills, your grammar corrections,
and your assistance in wrapping our little story up into a
picture perfect book for all of Mouse's friends!

DREAM BIG PUBLISHING, LLC, AUSTIN, TEXAS

Illustrations by Marcin Piwowarski

ISBN-13: 978-1-7331529-6-9